LON

HERE is a list for those who may wish to identify the London scenes Ludwig Bemelmans has pictured in this book.

Madeline's plane is flying over
the HOUSES OF PARLIAMENT
BIG BEN is just above the nose
WESTMINSTER ABBEY lies to the right
and the river THAMES is in the background

Miss Clavel and her charges look for Madeline and Pepito in
TRAFALGAR SQUARE beneath NELSON'S COLUMN

They also look near
WESTMINSTER ABBEY and ST JAMES'S PALACE

They rush past the DRURY LANE THEATRE near COVENT GARDEN
and finally find the two children and their horse
in ST JAMES'S PARK

They watch the procession march past
TOWER BRIDGE and on to the TOWER OF LONDON
with its YEOMEN OF THE GUARD

Onwards, past the VICTORIA MEMORIAL
facing BUCKINGHAM PALACE
until they reach the Palace itself

# MADELINE
## IN
# London

by

Ludwig Bemelmans

First published in the UK in 1962 by Andre Deutsch Ltd
This edition first published in 1996 by Scholastic Children's Books
Euston House, 24 Eversholt Street
London NW1 1DB
a division of Scholastic Ltd
www.scholastic.co.uk
London ~ New York ~ Toronto ~ Sydney ~ Auckland
Mexico City ~ New Delhi ~ Hong Kong

ISBN 978 1407 11062 2

13

Papers used by Scholastic Children's Books are made from wood
grown in sustainable forests.

In an old house
in Paris

that was covered
with vines

Lived twelve little girls
in two straight lines.

They left the house

at half past nine.

The smallest one
was Madeline.

In another old house
that stood next door

Lived Pepito,
the son of

the Spanish Ambassador.

An Ambassador doesn't
have to pay rent,
But he has to move
to wherever he's sent.

He took his family
and his hat;

They left for England—
all but the cat.

"I'm glad," said the cat.
"There goes that bad hat.
Let him annoy some other kitten
At the Embassy in Great Britain."
The little girls all cried: "Boo-hoo—
We'd like to go to London too."

In London Pepito just picked at his dinner,
Soon he grew thin and then he grew thinner—

And when he began to look like a stick
His mama said, "My, this boy looks sick.
I think Pepito is lonely for
Madeline and the little girls next door."

His papa called Paris. "Hello, Miss Clavel,
My little Pepito is not at all well.

"He misses you; and he's lonesome for
Madeline and the little girls next door.

"May we request the pleasure of your company—
There's plenty of room here at our embassy."

"Quick, darlings, pack your bags, and we'll get
Out to the airport and catch the next jet."

Fill the house with lovely flowers,

Fly our flags from all the towers.

For Pepito's birthday bake
The most wonderful birthday cake.

Place twelve beds in two straight lines.
The last one here will be Madeline's.

"Welcome to London, the weather's fine,
And it's exactly half past nine."

"Good Heavens," said Miss Clavel, "we've brought no toy
For his excellency's little boy!"
Said Madeline, "Everybody knows, of course,
He always said he craved a horse."
In their little purses and in Miss Clavel's bag
There wasn't enough money to buy the meanest nag.

But in London there's a place to get
A retired horse to keep as a pet.

And when they went to the place, they found
A horse that was gentle, strong, and sound.

Some poor old dobbins are made into glue,
But not this one—

Look, he's as good as new.

"Happy birthday, Pepito, happy birthday to you.

This lovely horse belongs to you."

Just then—"Tara, tara"—a trumpet blew
Suddenly outside, and off he flew
Over the wall to take his place at the head

Of the Queen's Life Guards, which he had always led
Before the Royal Society for the Protection of Horses
Had retired him from Her Majesty's Forces.

"Oh, dear! They've gone. Oh, what a pity!

Come, children, we'll find them in the city."

"Careful, girls, watch your feet.

Look right before you cross the street."

Oh, for a cup of tea and crumpets—

Hark, hark, there goes the sound of trumpets.

These birds have seen

all this before.

But they are glad

of an encore.

And so are the people—on ship…

and shore.

And now it's getting really grand.

Here comes the mascot and his band.

The people below are stout and loyal,

And those on the balcony mostly Royal.

The show is over, it's getting dark
In the city, in the park.
Dinner is waiting; we must be on time.
Now let's find Pepito and Madeline.

Well, isn't it lovely—they're standing sentry
Right here at the Whitehall entry.
That is the power and the beauty:
In England everyone does his duty!

Visiting is fun and gay—

Let's celebrate a lovely day.

Everyone had been well fed,

Everyone was in his bed.

Only one was forgotten, he'd been on his feet
All day long, without anything to eat.

In a cottage that was thatched,
Wearing trousers that were patched,
Lived the gardener, who loved flowers,
Especially in the morning hours,
When their faces, fresh with dew,
Smiled at him—"How DO you do?"

The gardener, who was never late,
Opened up the garden gate.

The gardener dropped his garden hose.

There wasn't a daisy or a rose.

"All my work and all my care
For nought! Oh, this is hard to bear.

"Where's my celery, carrots, tomatoes, my beans and peas?
And not an apple on my apple trees!"

Everybody had to cry.
Not a single eye was dry.

Oh, look who is lying there,
With his feet up in the air.

"I feel his breath, he's not dead yet.
Quick, Pepito, get the vet."

The vet said, "Don't worry, he's only asleep.
Help me get him on his feet.

"As a diet, there is nothing worse
Than green apples and roses for an old horse."
"Dear lady," said Miss Clavel, "we beg your pardon.
It seems our horse has eaten up your garden.

"A little sunshine, a little rain,
And it all will be the same again."
Pepito's mother said, "Quite so, quite so!
Still I'm afraid the horse must go."

Then Madeline cried, "I know what to do.
Pepito, let us take care of him for you."

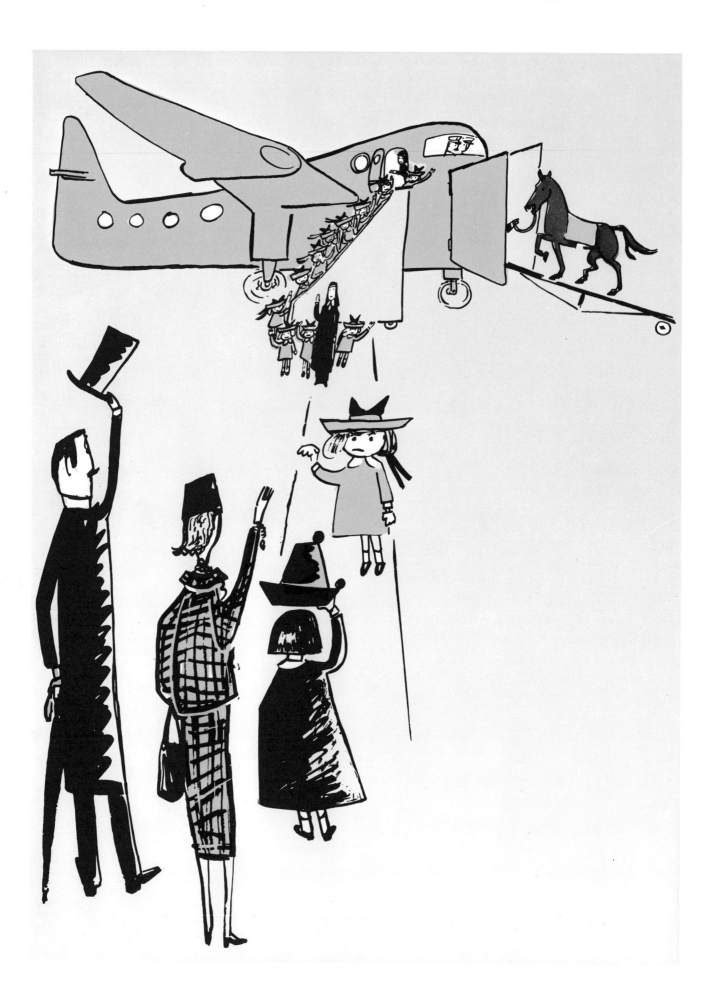

"Fasten your seat belts, in half an hour
You will see the Eiffel Tower."

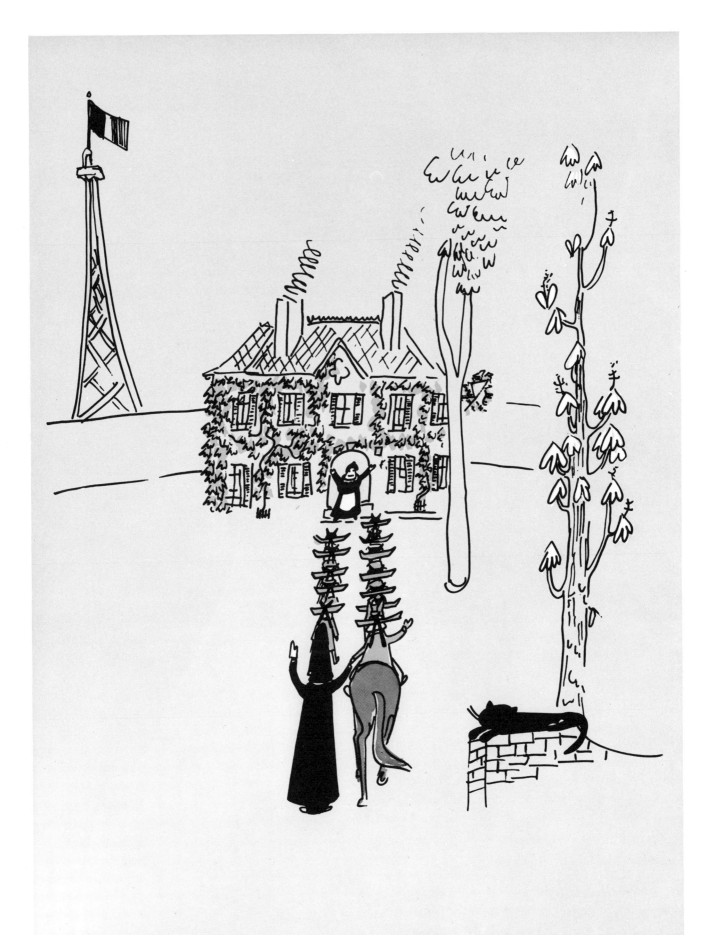

"Madeline, Madeline, where have you been?"
"We've been to London to see the Queen."

"At last," sighed Madeline, "we are able
To sit down without being thirteen at table."

They brushed his teeth and gave him bread,

And covered him up

and put him to bed.

"Good night, little girls,
Thank the Lord you are well.
And now go to sleep," said Miss Clavel.
And she turned out the light and closed the door.
There were twelve upstairs, and below one more.